NURSERY TALES AROUND the WORLD

Nursery Tales Around the World

Selected and Retold by JUDY SIERRA

Illustrated by STEFANO VITALE

CLARION BOOKS • New York

Clarion Books
a Houghton Mifflin Company imprint
215 Park Avenue South, New York, NY 10003
Text copyright © 1996 by Judy Sierra
Illustrations copyright © 1996 by Stefano Vitale

The illustrations for this book were executed in oil paint on wooden panels.
The text is set in 14/17.5-point Joanna.

For information about this and other Houghton Mifflin trade and reference books
and multimedia products, visit The Bookstore at Houghton Mifflin
on the World Wide Web at (http://www.hmco.com/trade/).

Printed in Singapore

Library of Congress Cataloging-in-Publication Data

Nursery tales around the world / [selected] by Judy Sierra ; illustrated by Stefano Vitale.
p.   cm.
Includes bibliographical and other "Notes on the tales" (p.).
Summary: Presents eighteen simple stories from international folklore, grouped around
six themes, such as "Runaway Cookies," "Slowpokes and Speedsters," and "Chain Tales."
Includes background information and storytelling hints.
ISBN 0-395-67894-3
1. Tales.   [1. Folklore.]   I. Sierra, Judy. II. Vitale, Stefano, ill.
PZ8.1.N799   1995
398.21—dc20
[E]   93-2068
CIP
AC

TWP   10   9   8   7   6   5   4   3   2   1

FOR HEATHER
—J.S.

FOR MY MOTHER
—S.V.

CONTENTS

INTRODUCTION

After lullabies and nursery rhymes, a young child's literary education naturally continues with stories. Parents are often in a rush to introduce their children to classics like *Winnie-the-Pooh* and *Charlotte's Web*. But not many two-, three-, and four-year-olds are ready for these. The age-old nursery tales from the oral tradition are more closely attuned to the needs of young listeners. Strong in rhythm, rhyme, and repetition, these stories are tailored to children's developing memory and imagination and to their unique way of viewing the world. Through these tales, children learn the basic story patterns of plot, theme, and character. And, while familiar folktales like "The Gingerbread Boy" may seem wildly silly to adults, a closer look will show that such tales often contain important messages about actions and their consequences.

The basic story lines of many nursery tales seem to have leaped across national and language boundaries, so that the North American "Gingerbread Boy" is very similar to a tale told in Russia called "The Bun," and a Scottish story known as "The Wee Bannock," and "The Pancake" from Sweden. Which one is the original? No one knows. What is certain is that variations of many folktales children love are found in many different cultures and languages.

A special quality of nursery tales is that even the longest are built from just a few basic elements—an easily remembered cast of characters, a few recurring chants and refrains, and a basic episode which is repeated until at last it is given a satisfying new twist and the story ends. These tales are easy to tell from memory at times when you need to entertain children—while traveling, for example. On such occasions, it's fun to make up new versions of old stories. Suppose that instead of a Gingerbread Boy there were a runaway pizza, or tortilla, or bagel. What would its journey be like? What hungry people and animals might it encounter? Who would be the one to eat it?

TIPS ON STORY READING

It is always a good idea to skim through a story before you read it aloud, so that you have an idea of the turns and twists of the plot and the personalities of the characters. Young children like to have stories presented in a dramatic fashion. If you enjoy being a ham, or have always wanted to create cartoon-style voices, this is your chance to perform for a very appreciative audience. However, don't be surprised when, like any great performer, you become a victim of your own success. It's quite normal for a preschool child to ask to hear the same story over and over, and to remember the exact words of the story and the precise way in which you read them the last time. Try to strike a balance between rereading favorite stories and reading new ones. After you finish a story, take time to look at the illustration together and comment on what is happening in it. This gives the child an opportunity to retell parts of the story, to ask questions, and to express emotional responses.

Children can't help but join in on cumulative refrains like the ones in these stories. Many of these refrains may also be sung (and probably were at one time), so feel free to make up your own melodies. Learning chants and refrains by heart gives children great satisfaction, and you are likely to overhear a child at odd times reciting parts of favorite stories: "I have run away from an old man, and an old woman. . . ."

The stories in this book are presented in groups of three, representing variations on one theme or plot. They are grouped in this way to highlight their similarities. Five-, six-, and seven-year-olds who have heard the tales many times may find new interest in discovering the similarities and differences among the three tales in a group. Also, these groupings offer an opportunity for preschool children to exercise independence by choosing the type of story they want to hear next.

Runaway Cookies

The tale of the runaway cookie is known and told in northern Europe, the British Isles, and North America. It vividly demonstrates the old proverb "Pride goeth before a fall." Far from being sad or fearful at the demise of the bun, pancake, or gingerbread boy, young children are delighted when the little treat is gobbled up. They know the story isn't true, and besides, they feel secure in the knowledge that *they* would never, ever have acted so foolishly.

THE GINGERBREAD MAN

United States

ONCE UPON A TIME there was a little old woman and a little old man, and they lived all alone in a little old house. They hadn't any little girls or any little boys at all. So one day the little old woman made a boy out of gingerbread. She made him a chocolate jacket, and put gumdrops on it for buttons. His eyes were made of fine fat currants, his mouth was made of rose-colored sugar, and he had a gay little cap of orange sugar candy. When the little old woman had rolled him out and dressed him up and pinched his gingerbread shoes into shape, she put him in a pan. Then she put the pan in the oven and shut the door, and she thought, "Now I shall have a little boy of my own."

When it was time for the Gingerbread Boy to be done,

3

she opened the oven door and pulled out the pan. Out jumped the little Gingerbread Boy on the floor, and away he ran—out the door and down the street! The little old woman and the little old man ran after him as fast as they could, but he just laughed and shouted,

> Run, run, as fast as you can,
> You can't catch me, I'm the Gingerbread Man!

And they couldn't catch him.

The little Gingerbread Boy ran on and on until he came to a cow by the roadside. "Stop, little Gingerbread Boy," said the cow. "I want to eat you."

The little Gingerbread Boy laughed and said,

> I have run away from a little old woman,
> And a little old man,
> And I can run away from you, I can!

And as the cow chased him, he looked over his shoulder and cried,

> Run, run, as fast as you can,
> You can't catch me, I'm the Gingerbread Man!

And the cow couldn't catch him.

The little Gingerbread Boy ran on and on and on till he came to a horse in the pasture. "Please stop, little Gingerbread Boy," said the horse. "You look very good to eat."

But the little Gingerbread Boy laughed out loud. "Oho! oho!" he said.

> I have run away from a little old woman,
> And a little old man,
> And a cow,
> And I can run away from you, I can!

And as the horse chased him, he looked over his shoulder and cried,

> Run, run, as fast as you can,
> You can't catch me, I'm the Gingerbread Man!

And the horse couldn't catch him.

By and by the little Gingerbread Boy came to a barn full of threshers. When the threshers smelled the Gingerbread Boy, they tried to pick him up, and said, "Don't run so fast, little Gingerbread Boy. You look very good to eat."

But the little Gingerbread Boy ran harder than ever, and as he ran he cried out,

5

I have run away from a little old woman,
And a little old man,
And a cow,
And a horse,
And I can run away from you, I can!

And when he found that he was ahead of the threshers, he turned and shouted back to them,

Run, run, as fast as you can,
You can't catch me, I'm the Gingerbread Man!

And the threshers couldn't catch him.

Then the little Gingerbread Boy ran faster than ever. He ran and ran until he came to a field full of mowers. When the mowers saw how fine he looked, they ran after him, calling out, "Wait a bit, wait a bit, little Gingerbread Boy, we wish to eat you!"

But the little Gingerbread Boy laughed harder than ever and ran like the wind. "Oho! Oho!" he said.

I have run away from a little old woman,
And a little old man,
And a cow,
And a horse,

And a barn full of threshers,
And I can run away from you, I can!

And when he found that he was ahead of the mowers, he turned and shouted back to them,

Run, run, as fast as you can,
You can't catch me, I'm the Gingerbread Man!

And the mowers couldn't catch him.

By this time the little Gingerbread Boy was so proud that he didn't think anybody could catch him. Pretty soon he saw a fox coming across a field. The fox looked at him and began to run. But the little Gingerbread Boy shouted across to him, "You can't catch me!" The fox began to run faster, and the little Gingerbread Boy ran faster, and as he ran he chuckled and said,

I have run away from a little old woman,
And a little old man,
And a cow,
And a horse,
And a barn full of threshers,
And a field full of mowers,
And I can run away from you, I can!

Run, run, as fast as you can,
You can't catch me, I'm the Gingerbread Man!

"Why," said the fox, "I would not catch you if I could. I would not think of disturbing you."

Just then the little Gingerbread Boy came to a river. He couldn't swim across, and he wanted to keep running away from the cow and the horse and the people.

"Jump on my tail, and I will take you across," said the fox.

So the little Gingerbread Boy jumped on the fox's tail, and the fox swam into the river.

When he was a little way from shore, the fox turned his head and said, "You are too heavy on my tail, little Gingerbread Boy. I fear I shall let you get wet. Jump on my back."

The little Gingerbread Boy jumped on his back.

A little farther out, the fox said, "I am afraid the water will cover you there. Jump on my shoulder."

The little Gingerbread Boy jumped on his shoulder.

In the middle of the river the fox said, "Oh dear, little Gingerbread Boy, my shoulder is sinking. Jump on my nose, and I can hold you out of the water."

So the little Gingerbread Boy jumped on his nose.

The minute the fox got on shore, he threw back his head, and gave a snap.

"Dear me!" said the little Gingerbread Boy. "I am a quarter gone!" The next minute he said, "My goodness gracious, I am three-quarters gone!"

And after that, the little Gingerbread Boy never said anything more at all.

THE PANCAKE

Norway

ONCE UPON A TIME there was a good woman who had seven hungry children, and she was frying a pancake for them. It was a sweet-milk pancake. There it lay in the pan, bubbling and frizzling, while the seven children stood around the stove and eyed it hungrily.

"Oh, give me a bit of pancake, Mother dear," said one of the children.

"Oh, darling Mother," said the second child.

"Oh, darling, good Mother," said the third.

"Oh, darling, good, nice Mother," said the fourth.

"Oh, darling, pretty, good, nice Mother," said the fifth.

"Oh, darling, pretty, good, nice, clever Mother," said the sixth.

"Oh, darling, pretty, good, nice, clever, sweet Mother," said the seventh.

So they all begged for the pancake, the one more sweetly than the other, because they were all so hungry.

"Yes, yes, children," the good woman said. "Just wait a bit till it turns itself."

The pancake was quite surprised to hear her say this. "Why, I shall turn myself then," it said. The pancake jumped up in the air and landed on its other side, where it sizzled a bit. Then up it jumped again, so high and so far that it landed on the floor. Then the pancake rolled out the door.

"Whoa, pancake! Stop, pancake!" cried the woman, and she chased after it with the frying pan in one hand and the ladle in the other. She ran as fast as she could, and her seven children ran after her.

"Stop that pancake! Stop that pancake!" they all shouted as they tried to grab ahold of it, but the pancake rolled on and on until they could no longer see it.

When it had rolled a bit farther, the pancake met a man.

"Good day, pancake," said the man.

"The same to you, manny-panny," said the pancake.

"Dear pancake, don't roll so fast. Stop awhile and let me take a bite of you."

But the pancake didn't stop, and as it rolled it called out,

I have rolled away from goody-poody,
And her seven squalling children,
And I shall roll away from you, too, manny-panny!

Then the pancake rolled on and on until it met a hen.
"Good day, pancake," said the hen.
"The same to you, henny-penny," said the pancake.
"Sweet pancake, don't roll so fast. Please stop awhile and let me have a peck at you."
But the pancake didn't stop, and as it rolled it called out,

I have rolled away from goody-poody,
And her seven squalling children,
And manny-panny,
And I shall roll away from you, too, henny-penny!

The pancake rolled on down the road like a wheel. Just then it met a duck.
"Good day, pancake," said the duck.
"The same to you, ducky-lucky," said the pancake.
"Pancake, dear, don't roll away so fast. Wait a bit so that I can eat you up."
But the pancake didn't stop, and as it rolled it called out,

I have rolled away from goody-poody,
And her seven squalling children,
And manny-panny,
And henny-penny,
And I shall roll away from you, too, ducky-lucky!

And the pancake rolled along faster than ever. Then it met a goose.

"Good day, pancake," said the goose.

"The same to you, goosey-poosey," said the pancake.

"Pancake dear, don't roll so quickly. Wait a minute and I'll eat you up."

But the pancake kept on rolling, and as it rolled it called out,

I have rolled away from goody-poody,
And her seven squalling children,
And manny-panny,
And henny-penny,
And ducky-lucky,
And I shall roll away from you, too, goosey-poosey!

When it had rolled a long way farther, the pancake came to the edge of a wood, and there stood a pig.

"Good day, pancake," said the pig.

"The same to you, piggy-wiggy," said the pancake.

"Don't be in such a hurry," said the pig. "The wood is dangerous, and we should walk together."

The pancake thought that might be true, and so it rolled along beside the pig for a bit. But when they had gone a ways, they came to a brook. The pig jumped right into the water and began to swim across.

"What about me? What about me?" cried the pancake.

"Oh, just you sit on my snout," said the pig, "and I'll carry you across."

So the pancake sat on the pig's snout.

The pig tossed the pancake up into the air, and—*ouf, ouf, ouf*—the pig swallowed the pancake in three bites.

And since the pancake went no further, this story can go no further, either.

THE BUN

Russia

ONCE THERE LIVED AN OLD MAN and an old woman. The old man asked the old woman to bake him a bun.

"What shall I make it from?" she asked. "We have no flour."

"Scrape the bottom of the flour bin and you will have enough," said the old man.

The old woman reached down and scraped the bottom of the flour bin until she had just enough flour to make one small, round bun. She mixed it with milk and baked it in butter, and she put the bun on the windowsill to cool. Suddenly the bun jumped up and rolled off the windowsill and onto the bench, and off the bench and onto the floor, and across the floor and out the door. On it rolled across the yard and out the gate and on and on and on.

17

The bun rolled along the road, and it met a hare.

"Little bun, little bun, let me eat you up!" said the hare.

"Don't eat me! Don't eat me! I will sing you a song." And the bun sang,

> I'm a bun! I'm a bun!
> I was scraped from the bin,
> I was mixed with milk,
> I was baked in butter.
> I ran away from Grandpa,
> I ran away from Grandma,
> And I will run away from you!

The bun rolled on faster, and the hare was left far behind. The bun rolled on and met a wolf.

"Little bun, little bun, I shall eat you up," said the wolf.

"Don't eat me, gray wolf!" said the bun. "I will sing a song for you." And the bun sang,

> I'm a bun! I'm a bun!
> I was scraped from the bin,
> I was mixed with milk,
> I was baked in butter.
> I ran away from Grandpa,

I ran away from Grandma,
I ran away from a hare,
And I will run away from you!

And the bun rolled faster, and the wolf was left far behind. The bun rolled on and met a bear.

"Little bun, little bun, I shall eat you up," the bear said.

"You'll never eat me, old bowlegged bear!" said the bun, and it sang,

I'm a bun! I'm a bun!
I was scraped from the bin,
I was mixed with milk,
I was baked in butter.
I ran away from Grandpa,
I ran away from Grandma,
I ran away from a hare,
I ran away from a wolf,
And I will run away from you!

And again the bun rolled faster, and left the bear far behind.

The bun rolled and rolled and met a fox. "Good day, little bun, how sweet you look," said the fox. And the bun sang,

I'm a bun! I'm a bun!
I was scraped from the bin,
I was mixed with milk,
I was baked in butter.
I ran away from Grandpa,
I ran away from Grandma,
I ran away from a hare,
I ran away from a wolf,
I ran away from a bear,
And I will run away from you!

"What a wonderful song," said the fox. "But little bun,
I am so old, I can't hear you very well. Please sit down on
my snout and sing your song again, louder this time."
The bun jumped on the fox's snout and sang,

I'm a bun! I'm a bun!
I was scraped from the bin,
I was mixed with milk,
I was baked in butter.
I ran away from Grandpa,
I ran away from Grandma,
I ran away from a hare,
I ran away from a wolf,
I ran away from a bear,
And I will run away from you!

"Thank you, little bun, for your wonderful song. How I would love to hear it again! Come now, sit on my tongue, and sing it one last time."

The fox stuck out her tongue. The bun foolishly jumped on it. *Snap!* The fox ate the little bun in one bite.

Incredible Appetites

These stories about swallowing an impossible series
of things are wildly improbable. Young children find
them side-splittingly funny. As children discover
how the real world works, they take great delight in
declaring that impossible things are true. In the following three tales, the impossible is carried to
ridiculous lengths. And yet, the observant adult will
find more than nonsense in these tales—a more
serious message about the dangers of an appetite,
of whatever sort, that is out of control.

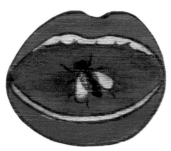

I KNOW AN OLD LADY
WHO SWALLOWED A FLY
United States

I KNOW AN OLD LADY who swallowed a fly.
I don't know why, but she swallowed a fly.
I guess she'll die.

I know an old lady who swallowed a spider;
It wiggled, and jiggled, and tickled inside her.
She swallowed the spider to catch the fly,
But I don't know why she swallowed the fly.
I guess she'll die.

I know an old lady who swallowed a bird—

How absurd to swallow a bird!
She swallowed the bird to catch the spider
That wiggled, and jiggled, and tickled inside her.
She swallowed the spider to catch the fly,
But I don't know why she swallowed the fly.
I guess she'll die.

I know an old lady who swallowed a cat—
Imagine that! She swallowed a cat.
She swallowed the cat to catch the bird,
She swallowed the bird to catch the spider
That wiggled, and jiggled, and tickled inside her.
She swallowed the spider to catch the fly,
But I don't know why she swallowed the fly.
I guess she'll die.

I know an old lady who swallowed a dog—
What a hog, to swallow a dog!
She swallowed the dog to catch the cat,
She swallowed the cat to catch the bird,
She swallowed the bird to catch the spider
That wiggled, and jiggled, and tickled inside her.
She swallowed the spider to catch the fly,
But I don't know why she swallowed the fly.
I guess she'll die.

I know an old lady who swallowed a goat—
She opened her throat, and in walked a goat!
She swallowed the goat to catch the dog,
She swallowed the dog to catch the cat,
She swallowed the cat to catch the bird,
She swallowed the bird to catch the spider
That wiggled, and jiggled, and tickled inside her.
She swallowed the spider to catch the fly,
But I don't know why she swallowed the fly.
I guess she'll die.

I know an old lady who swallowed a cow—
I don't know how, but she swallowed a cow!
She swallowed the cow to catch the goat,
She swallowed the goat to catch the dog,
She swallowed the dog to catch the cat,
She swallowed the cat to catch the bird,
She swallowed the bird to catch the spider
That wiggled, and jiggled, and tickled inside her.
She swallowed the spider to catch the fly.
But I don't know why she swallowed the fly,
I guess she'll die.

I know an old lady who swallowed a horse—
She's dead, of course.

27

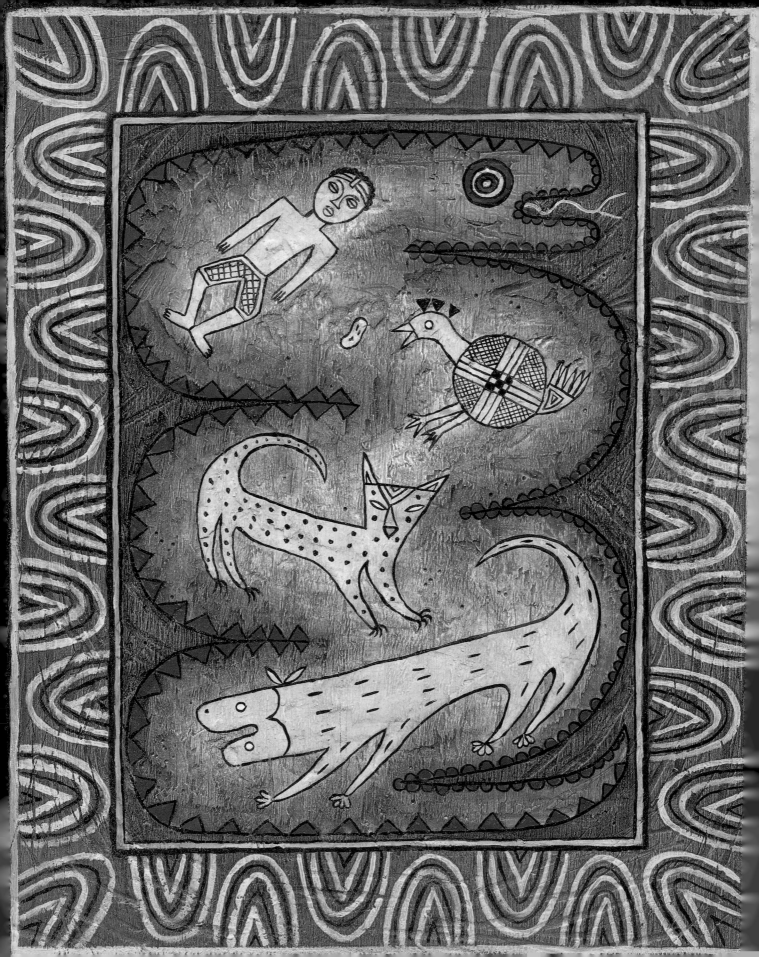

THE BOY WHO TRIED TO FOOL HIS FATHER

Zaire

ONE DAY, A BOY said to his father, "I am going to hide, and you won't be able to find me."

"Hide wherever you like," said his father. "I will find you." Then he went into the house to rest.

The boy saw a peanut lying on the ground, and he wished he could hide inside it. No sooner said than done; the boy found himself inside the peanut shell. He waited for his father to look for him.

Buk, buk, buk—a rooster came along and swallowed the peanut.

Rrrrrrr—wild bush cat came into the yard, and swallowed the rooster, and ran off into the thick brush.

Ruff! Ruff! A dog ran after that bush cat and swallowed it. Then the dog was thirsty, and went to the river for a drink.

Sssssss—a python crept up from behind, and swallowed the dog. Then the python fell in the river, and was caught in a fishnet.

Meanwhile, the boy's father had searched and searched for his son, but he couldn't find him. It was getting dark,

30

and he had to check his fishnets at the river. When the father pulled his first net up onto the bank, he found a python with a huge, swollen belly.

Inside the python, he found a dog.

Inside the dog, he found a bush cat.

Inside the bush cat, he found a rooster.

Inside the rooster, he found a peanut.

He broke open the peanut and out jumped his son.

That boy never tried to fool his father again!

THE CAT AND THE PARROT

India

ONCE THERE WAS A CAT AND A PARROT. And they agreed to ask each other to dinner, turn and turn about. First the cat would ask the parrot, then the parrot would invite the cat, and so on. It was the cat's turn first.

Now the cat was very mean. He provided nothing at all for dinner except a pint of milk, a little slice of fish, and a biscuit. The parrot was too polite to complain, but he did not have a very good time.

33

When it was his turn to invite the cat, he cooked a fine dinner. He had a roast of meat, a pot of tea, a basket of fruit, and, best of all, he baked a whole clothesbasketful of little cakes—little, brown, crispy, spicy cakes—oh, I should say as many as five hundred. And he put four hundred and ninety-eight of the cakes before the cat, keeping only two for himself.

Well, the cat ate the roast, and drank the tea, and sucked the fruit, and then he began on the pile of cakes. He ate all the four hundred and ninety-eight cakes, and then he looked round and said, "I'm hungry; haven't you anything to eat?"

"Why," said the parrot, "here are my two cakes if you want them."

The cat ate up the two cakes, and then he licked his chops and said, "I am beginning to get an appetite. Have you anything to eat?"

"Well, really!" said the parrot, who was rather angry. "I don't see anything more, unless you wish to eat me!" He thought the cat would be ashamed when he heard that. But the cat just looked at him and licked his chops again, and *slip! slop! gobble!* down his throat went the parrot!

Then the cat started down the street. An old woman was standing by, and she had seen the whole thing, and she was shocked that the cat should eat his friend. "Why, cat!" she said. "How dreadful of you to eat your friend the parrot!"

"Parrot, indeed!" said the cat. "What's a parrot to me? I've a great mind to eat you, too." And before you could say "Jack Robinson," *slip! slop! gobble!* down went the old woman.

Then the cat started down the road again, walking like this, because he felt so fine. Pretty soon he met a man driving a donkey. The man was beating the donkey to hurry him up, and when he saw the cat he said, "Get out of my way, cat; I'm in a hurry and my donkey might tread on you."

"Donkey, indeed!" said the cat. "Much I care for a donkey! I've eaten five hundred cakes, I've eaten my friend the parrot, I've eaten an old woman, so what's to keep me from eating a miserable man and a donkey?" And *slip! slop! gobble!* down went the old man and the donkey.

Then the cat walked on down the road jauntily, like this. After a little while, he met a procession. The king was at the head, walking proudly with his newly married bride, and behind him were his soldiers, marching, and behind them were ever and ever so many elephants, walking two by two. The king felt very kind to everybody, because he had just been married, and he said to the cat, "Get out of my way, kitty, get out of my way. My elephants might hurt you."

"Hurt me!" said the cat, shaking his fat sides. "Ho, ho! I've eaten five hundred cakes, I've eaten my friend the parrot, I've eaten an old woman, I've eaten a man and a donkey, so what's to keep me from eating a beggarly king?" And *slip! slop! gobble!* down went the king, down went the queen, down went the soldiers—and down went all the elephants.

Then the cat went on, more slowly. He had really had enough to eat now, but a little farther on he met two land crabs, scuttling along in the dust. "Get out of our way, kitty," they squeaked.

"Ho, ho, ho!" cried the cat in a terrible voice. "I've eaten five hundred cakes, I've eaten my friend the parrot, I've eaten an old woman, a man with a donkey, a king, his queen, his men-at-arms, and all his elephants, and now I'll eat you too." And *slip! slop! gobble!* down went the two land crabs.

When the land crabs got down inside, they began to look around. It was very dark, but they could see the poor king sitting in a corner with his bride on his arm. She had fainted. Near them were the men-at-arms, treading on one another's toes, and the elephants, still trying to form in twos, but they couldn't because there wasn't room. In the opposite corner sat the old woman, and near her stood the man and his donkey. But in the other corner was a great pile of cakes, and the parrot perched upon them, his feathers all drooping.

"Let's get to work!" said the land crabs. And, *snip*, *snap*, *snip*, *snap*, they began to make a little hole in the side with their sharp claws, *snip*, *snap*, *snip*, *snap*, till it was big enough to get through. Then out they scuttled.

Then out walked the king, carrying his bride. Out marched the men-at-arms. Out tramped the elephants, two by two. Out came the old man, beating his donkey. Out walked the old woman, scolding the cat. And last of all, out hopped the parrot, holding a cake in each claw (you remember, two cakes was all he wanted).

But the poor cat had to spend the whole day sewing up the hole in his coat!

THE VICTORY OF THE SMALLEST

It's only natural that children want to hear stories in which a small character triumphs. Cleverness and unique physical abilities allow tiny animals like ants, squirrels, and birds to outdo bears, goats, and giants. "The Ram in the Chile Patch" and "Sody Sallyraytus" were recorded and transcribed (and translated, in the case of "The Ram in the Chile Patch") to capture the oral style of traditional story-telling.

SODY SALLYRAYTUS

United States

ONE TIME THERE WAS AN OLD WOMAN and an old man and a little girl and a little boy—and a pet squirrel sittin' up on the fireboard. And one day the old woman wanted to bake some biscuits but she didn't have no sody, so she sent the little boy off to the store for some sody sallyraytus. The little boy he went trottin' on down the road singin', "Sody, sody, sody sallyraytus!" Trotted across the bridge and on to the store and got the sody sallyraytus, and started trottin' on back.

41

Got to the bridge and started across and an old bear stuck his head out from under it, says:

"I'LL EAT YOU UP—YOU AND YOUR SODY SAL-LYRAYTUS!"

So he swallered the little boy—him and his sody sallyraytus.

The old woman and the old man and the little girl and the pet squirrel they waited and they waited and they waited for the little boy, but he didn't come and didn't come, so fin'lly the old woman sent the little girl after the little boy. She skipped down the road and skipped across the bridge and on to the store, and the storekeeper told her the little boy had already been there and gone. So she started skippin' back, and when she got to the bridge the old bear stuck his head out—

"I EAT A LITTLE BOY, HIM AND HIS SODY SALLYRAY-TUS—AND I'LL EAT YOU TOO!"

So he swallered her down.

The old woman and the old man and the pet squirrel they waited and waited but the little girl didn't come and didn't come, so the old woman sent the old man after the little boy and the little girl. He walked on down the road, walked across the bridge—*Karump! Karump! Karump!*— and walked on till he came to the store, and the store-keeper told him the little boy and the little girl had already been there and gone.

"They must'a stopped somewhere 'side the road to play."

So the old man he started walkin' on back. Got to the bridge—

"I EAT A LITTLE BOY, HIM AND HIS SODY SALLYRAY-TUS, AND I EAT A LITTLE GIRL—AND I'LL EAT YOU, TOO!"

And the old bear reached and grabbed the old man and swallered him.

Well, the old woman and the pet squirrel they waited and waited but the old man didn't come and didn't come. So the old woman she put out a-hunchety-hunchin' down the road, crossed the bridge, got to the store, and the storekeeper told her, says, "That boy's already done been here and gone—him and the little girl and the old man, too."

So the old woman she went hunchin' on back—a-hunchety-hunchety-hunch. Got to the bridge—

"I EAT A LITTLE BOY, HIM AND HIS SODY SALLYRAY-TUS, AND I EAT A LITTLE GIRL, AND I EAT AN OLD MAN—AND I'LL EAT YOU, TOO!"

Reached out and grabbed her, and swallered her up.

Well, the pet squirrel he waited and he waited and he waited, and he went to runnin' back and forth up there on the fireboard, and he was gettin' hungrier and hungrier; so fin'lly he jumped down on the table, jumped off on the bench, and jumped to the floor. Shook his tail out behind him and out the door and down the road, just a-friskin'. Scuttered across the bridge and on in the store. R'ared up on his hindquarters and looked for the storekeeper, squarked a time or two, and when the storekeeper looked and saw him, the pet squirrel raised up on his tiptoes and asked him had he seen anything of the little boy or the little girl or the old man or the old woman.

"Law, yes! They all done already been here and gone. Surely they ain't *all* done stopped 'side the road to play."

So the pet squirrel he stretched his tail out behind 'im and frisked out the door. Frisked on over the bridge—

"I EAT A LITTLE BOY, HIM AND HIS SODY SALLYRAY-TUS, AND I EAT A LITTLE GIRL, AND I EAT AN OLD MAN, AND I EAT AN OLD WOMAN—AND I'LL EAT YOU, TOO!"

The little pet squirrel he stuck his tail straight up in the air and just chittered, but time the old bear made for him he was already scratchin' halfway up a tree. The old bear he went clamberin' up to get him. The squirrel got way out on a limb, and the old bear started out the limb after him. The squirrel he jumped and caught in the next tree.

"HUMPF! IF YOU CAN MAKE IT WITH YOUR LITTLE LEGS, I *KNOW* I CAN MAKE IT WITH MY BIG 'UNS!"

And the old bear tried to jump—didn't quite make it. Down he went, and when he hit the ground he split wide open.

The old woman stepped out, and the old man he stepped out, and the little girl jumped out, and the little boy he jumped out. And the old woman says, "Where's my sody sallyraytus?"

"Here," says the little boy, and he handed it to her.

So they went on back to the house and the pet squirrel he scooted on ahead of 'em, cloomb back up on the fireboard and curled his tail over his back and watched the old woman till she took the biscuits out the oven. So then she broke him off a chunk and blew on it till it wasn't too hot and handed it up to him. And he took it in his forepaws and turned it over and over and nibbled on it—and when he eat it up he leaned down and chittered for some more. And he was so hungry the old woman had to hand him chunks till he'd eat two whole biscuits.

THE RAM IN THE CHILE PATCH
Mexico

THERE WAS A LITTLE BOY who had a little patch of chile peppers. He tended it with the greatest care. That was what gave him his livelihood. And then one day a little ram got into it.

So the boy began, "Little ram, little ram, get out of that chile patch."

"You unmannerly boy, what are you about? Get out of here or I'll kick you out."

47

Finally he did try to get the little ram out, and the little ram, instead of leaving, gives him a kick and knocks the boy down. He struggles to his feet, and he goes away crying.

He meets a cow, and she says, "What's the matter, little boy?"

"¡Ay, *ay, ay!*" he says. "The little ram knocked me down."

"And why?"

"Because he's in my little chile patch."

"Just wait. I'll go get him out."

The cow comes up. "Moo, moo, moo! Little ram, little ram, get out of that chile patch."

"You big-horned cow, what are you about? Get out of here or I'll kick you out."

"Little ram, little ram, get out of that chile patch."

"You big-horned cow, what are you about? Get out of here or I'll kick you out."

Finally she did try. She tried to hook him with her horns, but the little ram turned around and kicked the cow out.

Then comes the dog, and he says, "I can get him out for sure." And he begins to bark. "Bow-wow-wow-wow! Little ram, little ram, get out of that chile patch."

"You shameless dog, what are you about? Get out of here or I'll kick you out."

"Little ram, little ram, get out of that chile patch."

"You shameless dog, what are you about? Get out of here or I'll kick you out."

The dog kept insisting and he got closer and closer, so the little ram gores him and leaves him the same as the cow.

Then comes the cock. He begins to crow, and he says, "Little ram, little ram, get out of that chile patch."

"You big eared cock, what are you about? Get out of here or I'll kick you out."

Finally the ram gores the cock and leaves him there with his legs in the air, and he goes away.

The ram kept on eating the little chile patch, and the boy was very sad because his chile patch was being eaten up. The burro comes, and he says, "Don't worry, little boy, I'll go get the ram out."

The burro begins, "Little ram, little ram, get out of that chile patch."

"You long-eared burro, what are you about? Get out of here or I'll kick you out."

At last the ram comes up close. He gores the burro and throws him out. And the boy sees that his little chile patch is almost gone, when a little ant comes, and then he says, "Little ant, little ant, if you would get the little ram out of my little chile patch for me, I would give you a lot of corn."

"How much will you give me?"

"I'll give you a bushel."

"That's too much."

"I'll give you half a bushel."

"That's too much."

"I'll give you a kilo."

"That's too much."

"I'll give you a handful."

"All right, then."

So the boy went, while the little ant got the ram out, he went and started grinding the corn so the little ant could carry it away without much trouble.

The ant went little by little, little by little, and climbed up one of the ram's little legs. She started to climb, and climbed and climbed until she got to his little behind.

She stings him and the ram jumps, it leaps and then begins to say, "Oh, my dear! Oh, my dear! She has stung me on the rear! Oh, my dear! Oh, my dear! She has stung me on the rear!"

And that is how they were able to get the little ram out.

ODON THE GIANT

Philippines

ONCE THERE LIVED A GIANT by the name of Odon, who went about crushing and stomping anyone who was smaller than he was, and there was nothing anyone could do to stop him. Finally, a little picoy bird came up with a plan. He announced that with four of the smallest creatures to help him, he could defeat Odon the Giant. The picoy bird asked a mosquito, a bedbug, a crab, and an eel to go with him to the giant's house, and they agreed.

The five companions set forth in a coconut shell, and together they paddled upriver to the place where Odon lived. All day they traveled. They arrived at the giant's house at sunset. Just as the picoy bird had expected, Odon was not at home—he was still out stomping and crushing. And so the picoy bird, the mosquito, the bedbug, the crab, and the eel quickly went up the bamboo ladder and into Odon's house.

Once they were inside, they followed the picoy bird's plan. The bedbug got into the giant's bed, the mosquito rested quietly on the back of the giant's rocking chair, the crab jumped into the washbasin, the eel curled up next to the doorway, and the picoy bird nestled down into the cool ashes at the edge of the fireplace.

Soon they heard the footsteps of the giant. He was climbing up the bamboo ladder to his house. Odon slowly walked inside, and sat down in his rocking chair with a giant sigh—"AAAAH." But no sooner had he sat down than—*bzzzzzzz*—the mosquito began to fly around his head, landing first in one ear—*bzzzzzzz*—then in the other ear—*bzzzzzzz*. Odon tried to slap the mosquito, but he only succeeded in hitting himself in the head.

Odon was very angry. "GRRRRRR!" he cried as he jumped into bed. He closed the mosquito netting tightly and lay down.

"OUCH! OUCH! What's that? Who is biting me?" Odon kicked and hit, but the bedbug kept on biting. The giant soon found himself wrapped up in the mosquito net, hitting himself again.

Odon ran across the room to the fireplace. He wanted to get a burning ember to light a lamp, so that he could see what sort of beast was attacking him.

But as he bent down to look in the fireplace, the picoy bird began to flap his small wings—*whirr, whirr, whirr*—making ashes fly into the giant's eyes. "ARRRRRR! MY EYES!" Odon ran to the washbasin and plunged his face into the water. Then the crab grabbed his lip and squeezed hard.

"HELP! HELP!" the giant cried. "MY HOUSE IS HAUNTED!" As Odon ran, screaming, toward the door, the slippery eel stretched his body across the threshold.

Odon the Giant stepped on the eel's tail—WHOOPS! He flew up high into the air, then he came down and landed on the ground with a *thud* that was heard for miles around. Odon the Giant ran away into the forest as fast as he could, and no one has seen him since.

CHAIN TALES

Chain tales describe a series of actions related by cause and effect. Some are realistic, like "This Is the House that Jack Built," while others are fantastic, like "Anansi and the Pig" or "The Rooster and the Mouse." The three chain tales that follow are narrated in a cumulative manner—the entire plot is retold each time a new story character is introduced. You may be tempted to skip the repetition in these stories, but don't! Young children love it, and will soon begin repeating the chains along with you.

THIS IS THE HOUSE THAT JACK BUILT

England

*T*HIS IS THE HOUSE that Jack built.

This is the malt
That lay in the house that Jack built.

This is the rat
That ate the malt
That lay in the house that Jack built.

This is the cat
That killed the rat
That ate the malt
That lay in the house that Jack built.

This is the dog
That worried the cat
That killed the rat
That ate the malt
That lay in the house that Jack built.

This is the cow with the crumpled horn,
That tossed the dog
That worried the cat
That killed the rat
That ate the malt
That lay in the house that Jack built.

This is the maiden all forlorn,
That milked the cow with the crumpled horn,
That tossed the dog
That worried the cat
That killed the rat
That ate the malt
That lay in the house that Jack built.

This is the man all tattered and torn,
That kissed the maiden all forlorn,
That milked the cow with the crumpled horn,
That tossed the dog

That worried the cat
That killed the rat
That ate the malt
That lay in the house that Jack built.

This is the priest all shaven and shorn,
That married the man all tattered and torn,
That kissed the maiden all forlorn,
That milked the cow with the crumpled horn,
That tossed the dog
That worried the cat
That killed the rat
That ate the malt
That lay in the house that Jack built.

This is the cock that crowed in the morn,
And wakened the priest all shaven and shorn,
That married the man all tattered and torn,
That kissed the maiden all forlorn,
That milked the cow with the crumpled horn,
That tossed the dog
That worried the cat
That killed the rat
That ate the malt
That lay in the house that Jack built.

This is the farmer sowing his corn,
That kept the cock that crowed in the morn,
That wakened the priest all shaven and shorn,
That married the man all tattered and torn,

That kissed the maiden all forlorn,
That milked the cow with the crumpled horn,
That tossed the dog
That worried the cat
That killed the rat
That ate the malt
That lay in the house that Jack built.

ANANSI AND THE PIG

Jamaica

ANANSI TOOK THE JOB to sweep the market. After he swept the market and got the pay, he bought a pig called "wee pig." On his way home he had to cross a stream. He couldn't get the pig across. He wouldn't carry it himself and he wouldn't pay anyone to assist him—wanted free help. So he saw a dog coming along. He said, "Br'er Dog, I beg you bite this pig, make this pig jump over the river, make Anansi get home."

Dog said no, couldn't do it.

He saw a stick coming along, said, "Do, Br'er Stick, I beg you lick this dog, make this dog bite this pig, make this pig jump over this river, make Anansi get home."

Stick said no, couldn't do it.

He see Fire, say, "Do, me good Fire, burn this stick, make this stick lick this dog, make this dog bite this pig, make this pig jump over this river, make Anansi get home."

Fire says no.

He sees Water. "Do, me good Water, I beg you out this fire, make this fire burn this stick, make this stick lick this dog, make this dog bite this pig, make this pig jump over the river, make Anansi get home."

Water said no.

He saw a cow coming. "Do, me good cow, drink this water, make this water out this fire, make this fire burn this stick, make this stick lick this dog, make this dog bite this pig, make this pig jump over this river, make Anansi get home."

Cow said no.

He saw a butcher coming. "Do, me good butcher, I beg you butcher this cow, make this cow drink this water, make this water out this fire, make this fire burn this stick, make this stick lick this dog, make this dog bite this pig, make this pig jump over this river, make Anansi get home!"

Butcher said no, wouldn't do it.

He sees Rope coming along. "Do, Br'er Rope, I beg you hang this butcher, make this butcher kill this cow, make this cow drink this water, make this water out this fire, make this fire burn this stick, make this stick lick this dog, make this dog bite this pig, make this pig jump over the river, make Anansi get home!"

Rope said no.

Saw a rat. Said, "Do, me good rat, gnaw this rope, make

this rope hang this butcher, make this butcher kill this cow, make this cow drink this water, make this water out this fire, make this fire burn this stick, make this stick lick this dog, make this dog bite this pig, make this pig jump over this river, make Anansi get home!"

Rat says no.

Saw Puss coming along. "Do, Br'er Puss, I beg you kill this rat, make this rat gnaw this rope, make this rope hang this butcher, make this butcher kill this cow, make this cow drink this water, make this water out this fire, make this fire burn this stick, make this stick lick this dog, make this dog bite this pig, make this pig jump over this river, make Anansi get home!"

Puss says, "Yes, I will kill your rat!"

Rat says, "Before you kill me, I will gnaw the rope!"

Rope says, "Before you gnaw me, I will hang the butcher!"

Butcher says, "Before you hang me, I will kill the cow!"

Cow says, "Before you kill me, I will drink the water!"

Water says, "Before you drink me, I will out the fire!"

Fire says, "Before you put me out, I will burn the stick!"

Stick says, "Before you burn me, I will lick the dog!"

Dog says, "Before you lick me, I will bite the pig!"

Pig says, "Before you bite me, I will jump over the river!"

So away went the pig over the river, and Anansi got him home safe and sound.

THE ROOSTER AND THE MOUSE

Italy

ONCE UPON A TIME there lived a rooster and a mouse. One day the mouse said to the rooster, "Shall we go and eat some nuts from yonder tree?"

"Certainly," the rooster replied.

So they both went to the tree, and the mouse climbed up the trunk, scampered out on a branch, and began to eat. The poor rooster flapped his wings, and flapped his wings, but he could not fly high enough to reach the branch.

"Friend mouse, do you know what I want you to do?" said the rooster. "Throw me down a nut."

The mouse threw down a nut, and it hit the rooster on the head and gave him a nasty bump. So poor rooster, with his head nearly broken, went to an old woman to get a rag for a bandage.

"Auntie, give me a bandage to cure my head."

"I will," said the woman, "if you will give me two hairs from a dog's back."

The rooster went away and found a dog.

> Dog, give me two hairs,
> The hairs I will give to the old woman,
> The old woman will give me a rag for a bandage
>   to cure my head.

"I will give you the hairs," said the dog, "if you will give me a little bread."

The rooster went to the baker and said

> Baker, give me bread,
> The bread I will give to the dog,
> The hairs I will give to the old woman,
> The old woman will give me a rag for a bandage
>   to cure my head.

The baker answered, "I will not give you bread unless you give me some wood."

The rooster went to the forest.

> Forest, give me some wood,
> The wood I will carry to the baker,
> The baker will give me some bread,

The bread I will give to the dog,
The hairs I will give to the old woman,
The old woman will give me a rag for a bandage
    to cure my head.

The forest answered, "If you will bring me a little water, I will give you some wood."
The rooster went to the fountain.

Fountain, give me water,
Water I will carry to the forest,
Forest will give me wood,
The wood I will carry to the baker,
The baker will give me some bread,
The bread I will give to the dog,
The hairs I will give to the old woman,
The old woman will give me a rag for a bandage
    to cure my head.

The fountain gave the rooster water, the water he carried to the forest, the forest gave him wood, the wood he carried to the baker, the baker gave him bread, the bread he gave to the dog, the dog gave him two hairs from his back, the hairs he carried to the old woman, the old woman gave him a rag for a bandage, and the rooster cured his head.

SLOWPOKES AND SPEEDSTERS

The race between a fast animal and a slow one is one of the most widespread folktale themes in the world. The plot of the Aesop's fable, in which the hare takes a nap and unwillingly lets the tortoise win, is scarcely ever found in oral tradition. In oral versions, the slowpokes are more resourceful, though not as honest as Aesop's tortoise. There are two major oral plots. In one, along the lines of "The Coyote and the Rabbit," the slower animal's look-alike relatives station themselves at intervals along the racecourse and trick the fast runner into thinking it sees only one opponent. In the other type, represented here by "The Fox and the Crab," the slower animal hitches a ride, undetected, on the the body of the speedster.

THE HARE AND THE TORTOISE

Greece

ONCE THE HARE WAS BRAGGING to all the other animals about how fast he was. "When I run full speed," he boasted, "no one can beat me. I challenge anyone here to race with me."

All were silent, until a small, quiet voice was heard. "I accept your challenge," said the tortoise.

"What a good joke!" cried the hare. I could dance circles around you all the way to the finish line."

"Save your boasting until after the race is over," the tortoise replied. "Shall we begin?"

And so a course was marked off, and the signal was given to begin. The hare dashed out of sight, but soon he stopped, and to show his contempt of the tortoise, he lay down for a nap.

The tortoise plodded on and on, never stopping to rest. When the hare awoke from his nap, he saw the tortoise in the distance, just about to cross the finish line. The hare could not get there in time to win.

It was the tortoise who was the victor, and who had the last word: "Slow and steady wins the race."

THE COYOTE AND THE RABBIT

United States, Native American: Pueblo

A COTTONTAIL RABBIT WAS SITTING just inside the door of his house one day, when along came a hungry coyote.

"What are you thinking, little friend?" the coyote asked the rabbit.

"I have just been wondering why some animals have large tails, like you, friend coyote, while others like me have practically no tail. Doesn't your long tail slow you down when you run?"

"Not at all," answered the coyote. "I can run faster than any other animal. No one has ever beaten me in a race."

"Perhaps you would like to race me, then," said the rabbit.

"Yes, indeed," answered the coyote. "Let us race to the four corners of the world. The winner of the race shall eat the loser."

The rabbit agreed. "In four days we shall run," he said.

The coyote went home happily, thinking about a tasty rabbit dinner. The cottontail quickly sent for all his relatives from the four corners of the world, and together they made plans for the race.

When the fourth day came, the coyote appeared at the door to the rabbit's house. "Friend, why should we run and tire ourselves out? Just let me eat you now."

"No," said the rabbit. "Let us race to the four corners of the world. I will race underground, of course, for I can run faster that way."

The two runners stood side by side, and then off they ran, the coyote across the mesa, the rabbit down into his burrow.

The coyote ran east for many days and saw nothing of the cottontail, but just as he came to the eastern edge of the world, up jumped a rabbit from a hole in the ground. "So, friend coyote! We've arrived at the same time!" cried the rabbit, and he dived into the hole, kicking dirt up into the air.

"Ai!" cried the coyote. "I wish I could run under the ground like that, for it seems very easy." He did not know that it was the uncle of the cottontail who had spoken to him.

The coyote ran harder, and after many days he came to the northern edge of the world. As he was about to turn to the west, up sprang a rabbit from a hole just in front of him.

"Ha!" shouted the rabbit. "I am still ahead of you." The rabbit disappeared down into the hole, kicking dirt into the face of the astonished coyote.

The coyote sped toward the west. But when he reached the western edge of the world, up popped a cottontail. "Slowpoke! Slowpoke!" the rabbit taunted him.

The coyote turned and ran even harder, but when he reached the south, what did he see? Poking out of a hole in the ground was the head of a rabbit. "I've been waiting for you," the cottontail said (this was a cousin of the first rabbit).

The coyote half-ran and half-limped back to the starting point of the race, where that cottontail rabbit was waiting for him, looking calm and refreshed.

"Now it is clear," said the rabbit, "that short tails are better for running with than long tails. And even though you are tough, come here and I will eat you."

The coyote turned and ran as fast and as far as he could, with his tail tucked firmly between his legs. Meanwhile, that cottontail and all his relatives had a good laugh at the trick they had played on the coyote.

THE FOX AND THE CRAB

China

A FOX ONCE WENT TO DRINK from the river, and there he saw a crab.

"Miserable little thing, do you ever run?" asked the fox.

"Yes," replied the crab. "Often I run from the river up to the grass and back again."

"Why, that's not really running," said the fox haughtily. "If I had as many legs as you do, I would run faster and farther than the wind. You are a stupid, slow creature."

81

"I believe that it is your tail that makes you such a fast runner," said the crab. "If you would tie down your tail, I believe I could beat you in a race."

The fox laughed at the idea of racing with the crab, but he agreed to do so. He also agreed that the crab could tie a weight to the end of his bushy tail.

"After I put this weight on your tail, I will call out 'Ready,' and we will start," said the crab.

The fox stood still. The crab went behind him and grabbed his tail with its claws.

"Ready!" the crab cried, and the fox began to run as fast as he could. On and on he went, and when he was too tired to run any farther, he turned around to have a look at the crab, thinking the tiny creature was far behind him. No crab was in sight.

Quickly, the crab let go of the fox's tail and called out, "So you have finally gotten here, brother fox? I thought you could run faster than I!"

The fox turned, and there, ahead of him on the path, was the crab. The fox hung his head in shame, and crept away.

Fooling the Big Bad Wolf

Adults sometimes feel hesitant about reading stories that feature characters like wolves to children, for fear of frightening them. Many storytellers and psychologists believe, however, that folktales like the three that follow help children overcome fears they already have. Young children take great pleasure in hearing about the triumph of good over evil, and ask for these stories again and again. In the following stories of fooling the big bad wolf, small, weak characters overcome the wolf by their own wits. This is how most oral tales unfold, unlike the well-known Charles Perrault story, "Red Riding Hood," in which the child is a helpless victim who must be rescued.

THE GUNNY WOLF

United States: African-American

A MAN AND HIS LITTLE DAUGHTER lived alone near the edge of the forest. Now, that man knew there were wolves in the forest, so he built a fence around the house, and told his little daughter she must on no account go outside the gate while he was away.

One morning when he had gone away, the little girl

was hunting for flowers, and she thought it would do no harm just to peep through the gate. As she did so, she saw a little flower so near that she stepped outside the gate to pick it. Then she saw another flower just a little ways off, and she picked that one too. She saw another, and another, and little by little she walked farther and farther away from home. And as she walked, she sang a song:

> Tray-bla,
>> Tray-bla,
>>> Kum-kwa,
>>>> Ki-mo.

All of a sudden she heard a noise. She stopped picking flowers, and looked up, and what should she see but a great big gunny wolf. The gunny wolf said, "Sing me that good, sweet song again."
So the little girl sang,

> Tray-bla,
>> Tray-bla,
>>> Kum-kwa,
>>>> Ki-mo.

And the gunny wolf lay down, and fell asleep.

Pit-a-pat,
> Pit-a-pat,
>> Pit-a-pat,

the little girl tiptocd away.
    But the gunny wolf woke up!

Hunk-a-cha!
> Hunk-a-cha!
>> Hunk-a-cha!

he ran after the little girl, and when he caught her he said,
"Sing me that good, sweet song again."
    So the little girl sang,

Tray-bla,
> Tray-bla,
>> Kum-kwa,
>>> Ki-mo.

And the gunny wolf lay down, and fell asleep.

Pit-a-pat,
> Pit-a-pat,
>> Pit-a-pat,

the little girl tiptoed away, and she was almost to the front gate when the gunny wolf woke up!

     Hunk-a-cha!
         Hunk-a-cha!
             Hunk-a-cha!

he ran after the little girl, and when he caught her he said, "Sing me that good, sweet song again."
  So the little girl sang,

     Tray-bla,
         Tray-bla,
             Kum-kwa,
                 Ki-mo.

And the gunny wolf lay down, and fell asleep.

     Pit-a-pat,
         Pit-a-pat,
             Pit-a-pat,
     Pit-a-pat,
         Pit-a-pat,
             Pit-a-pat,

the little girl tiptoed all the way home, and she closed the gate, and went inside the house, and locked the door, and after that, she stayed away from the woods where the gunny wolf lived.

GROUNDHOG'S DANCE

United States, Native American: Cherokee

ONCE, SEVEN WOLVES caught a fat little groundhog.

"Now we'll eat you," the seven wolves said.

"Tsk, tsk, tsk," scolded the groundhog. "When you find good food, you should dance before you eat it, the way people do."

"Of course," said the seven wolves. "We will dance, the way people do." They ran around and kicked their feet, but they looked so foolish!

"No! No!" the groundhog shouted. "That is *not* the way to dance. Because you are such bad dancers, I will have to teach you how to do it. I will sing, and you will dance, dance, dance away from me. When I say the word

'Yu,' you run toward me. Then when I start to sing again, you dance, dance, dance away. Understand?"

"Yes," said the seven wolves, and they nodded their heads happily. "Go ahead and sing."

The groundhog sang,

> Ha wi ye-a hi,
> Ya ha wi ye-a hi,
> Ha wi ye-a hi,
> Ya ha wi ye-a hi.

The wolves kept dancing away, farther, farther, farther away.

"*Yu!*" shouted the groundhog.

The seven wolves ran toward the groundhog, but before they reached him, he began to sing,

> Ha wi ye-a hi,
> Ya ha wi ye-a hi,
> Ha wi ye-a hi,
> Ya ha wi ye-a hi.

The seven wolves danced away, farther, farther, farther, farther away.

"*Yu!*" shouted the groundhog.

The seven wolves ran toward the groundhog, but before they caught him, he began to sing,

> Ha wi ye-a hi,
> Ya ha wi ye-a hi,
> Ha wi ye-a hi,
> Ya ha wi ye-a hi.

On and on he sang,

> Ha wi ye-a hi,
> Ya ha wi ye-a hi,
> Ha wi ye-a hi,
> Ya ha wi ye-a hi.

When the seven wolves had danced very, very, very far away, the groundhog ran as fast as he could to the old tree stump that hid the entrance to his hole. Just before he jumped down into his burrow, the groundhog shouted as loud as he could—"YU!"

When the wolves got to his burrow, just the tip of the groundhog's long bushy tail was sticking out. The first wolf bit the groundhog's tail, then gave it such a hard pull that it broke off. And the groundhog's tail has been short ever since.

THE THREE PIGS

England

Once upon a time when pigs spoke rhyme
And monkeys chewed tobacco,
And hens took snuff to make them tough,
And ducks went quack, quack, quack, O!

THERE WAS AN OLD SOW with three little pigs, and as she had not enough to keep them, she sent them out to seek their fortune.

The first that went off met a man with a bundle of straw, and said to him, "Please, man, give me that straw to build me a house," which the man did, and the little pig built a house with it.

Along came a wolf, and knocked at the door, and said, "Little pig, little pig, let me come in."

To which the pig answered, "No, no, not by the hair of my chinny chin chin."

The wolf then answered to that, "Then I'll huff, and I'll puff, and I'll blow your house in."

So he huffed, and he puffed, and he blew his house in, and ate up the little pig.

The second little pig met a man with a bundle of sticks, and said, "Please, man, give me those sticks to build a house," which the man did, and the pig built his house.

Then along came the wolf, and said, "Little pig, little pig, let me come in."

"No, no, not by the hair of my chinny chin chin."

"Then I'll huff, and I'll puff, and I'll blow your house in."

So he huffed, and he puffed, and he puffed, and he huffed, and at last he blew the house down, and he ate up the little pig.

The third little pig met a man with a load of bricks, and said, "Please, man, give me those bricks to build a house with." So the man gave him the bricks, and he built his house with them.

So the wolf came, as he did to the other little pigs, and said, "Little pig, little pig, let me come in."

"No, no, not by the hair of my chinny chin chin."

"Then I'll huff, and I'll puff, and I'll blow your house in."

Well, he huffed, and he puffed, and he huffed and he puffed, and he puffed and huffed. But he could not get the house down.

When he found that he could not, with all his huffing and puffing, blow the house down, he said, "Little pig, I know where there is a nice field of turnips."

"Where?" said the little pig.

"Oh, Mr. Smith's field, and if you will be ready tomorrow morning I will call for you, and we will go together and get some for dinner."

"Very well," said the little pig, "I will be ready. What time do you mean to go?"

"Oh, at six o'clock."

Well, the little pig got up at five and got the turnips before the wolf came at six and said, "Little pig, are you ready?"

The little pig said, "Ready! I have gone and come back again, and got a nice potful of turnips for dinner."

The wolf felt very angry at this, but thought that he would get the better of the little pig somehow or other, so he said, "Little pig, I know where there is a nice apple tree."

"Where?" said the pig.

"Down at Merry Garden," replied the wolf, "and if you will not deceive me I will come for you at five o'clock tomorrow and we will get some apples."

Well, the little pig bustled up the next morning at four

o'clock, and went off for the apples, hoping to get back before the wolf came. But he had farther to go, and had to climb the tree, so that just as he was coming down from it, he saw the wolf coming, which, as you may suppose, frightened him very much.

When the wolf came up he said, "Little pig . . . WHAT! Are you here before me? Are they nice apples?"

"Yes, very," said the little pig. "I will throw you down one."

And he threw it so far that while the wolf was gone to pick it up, the little pig jumped down and ran home.

The next day the wolf came again and said to the little pig, "Little pig, there is a fair at Shanklin this afternoon. Will you go?"

"Oh yes," said the pig. "I will go. What time will you be ready?"

"At three," said the wolf.

So the little pig went off early, as usual, and got to the fair, and bought a butter churn, which he was going home with when he saw the wolf coming. Then he did not know what to do. So he got into the churn to hide, and turned it around, and it rolled down the hill with the pig in it. This frightened the wolf so much that he ran home without going to the fair. He went to the little pig's house and told him how frightened he had been by the great round thing that came down the hill past him.

Then the little pig said, "Hah! I frightened you, then. I had been to the fair and bought a butter churn, and when I saw you, I got into it and rolled down the hill."

Then the wolf was very angry indeed, and declared he would eat up the little pig, and that he would get down the chimney after him. When the little pig saw what the wolf was about, he hung on the pot full of water, and made up a blazing fire, and, just as the wolf was coming down, took off the cover, and in fell the wolf. So the little pig put on the cover again in an instant, boiled him up, and ate him for supper, and lived happy ever afterward.

About the Tales

RETELLINGS

The written source for each tale in this collection is given below, along with an indication of whether I have retold that particular text. In the case of tales I have noted as "slightly retold," I have simply updated some of the vocabulary.

Retelling folktales from printed sources is often necessary, usually because they have lost their oral qualities in the process of being transcribed, translated, and edited. Some tale texts in books are merely plot summaries, while others have been rewritten in an awkward style by collectors who were neither experienced writers nor storytellers. For example, the English text of "Odon the Giant" contains such sentences as, "The part of the crab now presented itself, for when sight was denied to the giant by the ashes of the stove, he resorted to the basin to wash them off"—scarcely good storytelling style. Early collectors of folktales routinely eliminated features of oral tales that live audiences love, such as repetition.

When the folktale collector or editor knew the language and traditions of the storyteller, a good oral style was often achieved, as in the case of tales in this collection by Peter Christen Asbjørnsen and Jørgen Moe (translated nicely into English by George Webbe Dasent) and by Richard Chase. Three tales in this book, "Sody Sallyratus," "The Ram in the Chile Patch," and "Anansi and the Pig," were transcribed in language that reflects oral style of storytellers whose names are recorded and passed along by the collectors, something that was all too frequently not done. True oral style is usually ungrammatical by written standards (even when the storyteller is educated), and often shifts back and forth between present and past tense.

In retelling the tales that I find to be good stories though lacking in read-aloud appeal, I have relied upon my knowledge of other tales from the same culture, and my long experience telling stories to children. I have not changed the substance of the tales, but rather the style of the English retelling.

NOTES

The following notes include references to tale types, variants, and motifs. *Tale type* is a way of grouping together folktales that have similar plots, characters, and themes. Folklorists Antti Aarne and Stith Thompson created this classification system. Their book, *The Types of the Folktale*, catalogues the different languages and culture areas in which certain plot types had been recorded. The book is not complete (it hasn't been updated since 1961, and it focuses chiefly on tales from Europe and India) but it is still very useful in studying folktales.

The whole idea of tale type raises the question of why the same basic tales are so widely told. Did they originate in one place, then spread? Or did they arise spontaneously in many cultures? So far, this remains an unsolved mystery. Folklorists refer to differing regional versions of a tale type as *variants*. Hundreds of variants in dozens of languages have been reported for Tale Type 510A, *Cinderella*, for example.

Motifs are small units of narrative that are found in more than one tale. They have been catalogued by Stith Thompson in his six-volume *Motif-Index of Folk-Literature*. A motif can be a certain type of episode, a unique character, or a striking image or action that is part of the toolbox of story-tellers in one or several cultures. An example of a widespread motif is K741, *Capture by tar baby*.

THE GINGERBREAD MAN/*United States*

Source: Sara Cone Bryant, *Stories to Tell to Children*. Bryant was told the story as a child. Slightly retold.

All three tales of runaway cookies included in this book are variants of

Tale Type 2025, *The Fleeing Pancake*. Aarne and Thompson mention variants from Lithuania, Latvia, Sweden, Norway, Denmark, Scotland, Ireland, Germany, Slovenia, Russia, England, and the United States.

Other runaways are round rollers, but the Gingerbread Man has legs. This variant from the United States first appeared in print in the children's magazine *Saint Nicholas* in May 1875.

THE PANCAKE/*Norway*

Source: George Webbe Dasent, *Tales from the Fjeld*. Slightly retold.

"Goody," short for "goodwife," is an old English way of addressing a married woman, like the modern "Mrs." The rhyming nonsense names of the characters in this tale recall the story of Chicken Little (also known as Henny Penny). In the original Norwegian text of this tale, the characters also have rhyming names: *kone krone* (the woman), *mand brand* (the man), *høne pøne* (the hen), *ande vande* (the duck), and *gasse vasse* (the goose).

THE BUN/*Russia*

Source: Aleksandr Afanas'ev, *Russian Folk-Tales* Retold.

I KNOW AN OLD LADY WHO SWALLOWED A FLY/*United States*

Source: Traditional.

This rhyme is well known in the United States as a chant and as a song. Aarne and Thompson do not assign it a tale type number, but Thompson lists Motif Z49.14, *The little old lady who swallowed a fly*, and cites only this version. The progressively bigger and bigger animals that are swallowed, and the rhymes made with their names, make "I Know an Old Lady Who Swallowed a Fly" very easy to remember. The lady's adventures could be considered a tall tale, though I prefer to think of it as a numbskull story in which the heroine's actions seem logical, but prove fatally flawed when applied in real life.

THE BOY WHO TRIED TO FOOL HIS FATHER/*Zaire*

Source: John H. Weeks, *Congo Life and Folklore*. Retold.

    This tale is not classified by tale type in *The Types of the Folktale*. Thompson lists Motif Z43.5, *Boy changes self to nut; fowl eats nut; bush cat eats fowl; dog eats cat; dog swallowed by python.* He cites only this tale as an example of the motif.

THE CAT AND THE PARROT/*India*

Source: Sara Cone Bryant, *How to Tell Stories to Children*. Slightly retold.

    Aarne and Thompson report variants of Tale Type 2027, *The Fat Cat*, from Sweden, Denmark, India, and the United States. Danish folklorist Bengt Holbek compared twenty oral tellings of this tale type collected in Denmark and found that the kinds of people, animals, and objects the cat swallowed varied widely from tale to tale, suggesting that there is no standard version of this tale, even within a small language area like Denmark. The things swallowed, however, always reflected a pattern of "mounting ambition and abrupt downfall" on the part of the cat. The identity of the creature who finally overcomes the cat also varied widely, and cutting open the cat's belly could be achieved from inside or outside, as long as the victor possessed a sharp object (for example a sword, an axe, or a goat's horns).

SODY SALLYRAYTUS/*United States*

Source: Richard Chase, *Grandfather Tales*. Collected from Kena Adams of

Wise County, Virginia, and retold by Chase. Reprinted with permission.

This tale does not conform to any one tale type. The beginning resembles Tale Type 122E, *Wait for the Fat Goat (The Three Billy-goats Gruff)*, and it also resembles Tale Type 2027, *The Fat Cat*, although this tale focuses on the people swallowed rather than on the swallowing monster. In *Twenty Tellable Tales*, folklorist and storyteller Margaret Read MacDonald describes how she changes the ending of this tale when she tells it: "I became so attached to the old bear . . . I have just sewn him up again and sent him on his way" (88). Comparison of many tellings of one tale type confirms that the punishment of a villain in a folktale is very much the storyteller's (and indirectly the listeners') choice. The climax of a tale (in this instance, the bear bursting open) is seldom changed, however. Soda saleratus is the name of a chemical compound formerly used in baking breads and biscuits, in the same way that baking soda is used today. The fireboard is the shelf above a fireplace, usually called the mantelpiece.

THE RAM IN THE CHILE PATCH/*Mexico*

Source: Américo Paredes, *Folktales of Mexico*. Collected by Stanley L. Robe in Tepatitlán, Jalisco. Told by María del Refugio Gonzalez. Slightly retold with permission.

Aarne and Thompson indicate variants of Tale Type 2015, *The Goat who Would not Go Home*, from Finland, Sweden, Norway, France, Spain, Holland, Belgium, Italy, Hungary, Slovenia, Yugoslavia, Russia, Turkey, and Spanish America.

ODON THE GIANT/*Philippines*

Source: Henry Otley Beyer, "Ethnography of the Bisayan Peoples." Retold.
Variants of this tale, Tale Type 130, *The Animals in Night Quarters*, are found widely in Europe and Asia and among European Americans. The

Grimms' "Bremen Town Musicians" is a variant of this tale type, as is the Chinese tale "The Terrible Nung Gwama." The characters in the tale may be animals or animated objects, or both, and they may be led by either a human or an animal. In the Grimms' "Mister Korbes" the characters are a cock, a hen, a cat, a millstone, an egg, a duck, a pin, and a needle.

THIS IS THE HOUSE THAT JACK BUILT/*England*

Source: Traditional.

Aarne and Thompson cite variants of Tale Type 2035, *House That Jack Built*, from India, Africa, and Europe. This is a realistic chain of events that does not reach a climax or resolution; it appears, rather, that all possible rhymes were exhausted.

ANANSI AND THE PIG/*Jamaica*

Source: Martha Warren Beckwith, "Jamaica Anansi Stories." Told by Moses Hendricks of Mandeville. Reprinted with permission.

This is a variant of Tale Type 2030, *The Old Woman and her Pig*, which has been very widely recorded from Ireland to India and Indonesia, as well as in European-American and African-American variations. The tale is set up through a chain of threats, which then reverses when the person seeking a favor makes an exchange with one member of the chain, setting off a "chain reaction" resulting in the achievement of the initial goal.

Anansi is a trickster hero of West African and Afro-Caribbean storytelling tradition, and is usually identified as a spider.

THE ROOSTER AND THE MOUSE/*Italy*

Source: Thomas Frederick Crane, *Italian Popular Tales*. Retold.

Aarne and Thompson report variants of Tale Type 2032, *The Cock's*

Whiskers, from Europe, Turkey, and Armenia. Variants from Central America, India, and Southeast Asia have also been included in recent anthologies. This tale often begins with an animal losing part of its body, such as a tail, then trying to get it back. This type of chain is a chain of favors, and the chain ends when the seeker has something of value to offer to one of the tale's characters, setting off the chain reaction. Tales of this type do not always end happily, though. In the Russian tale "The Death of the Cock," for example, fetching the medicine takes so long that the patient dies.

THE HARE AND THE TORTOISE/*Greece*

Source: Aesop.

Catalogued by Aarne and Thompson as Tale Type 275A, *Hare and Tortoise Race: Sleeping Hare*, this plot type is not widely found in oral tradition. The moral given by Aesop is contradicted by the facts of the tale, for the tortoise's victory depends upon the hare's overconfidence. Slow and steady wins the race only under certain conditions, and this tale serves more as a warning to the swift than as advice to the slow.

THE COYOTE AND THE RABBIT/*Native American · Pueblo*

Source: Charles F. Lummis, *Pueblo Indian Folk-Stories*. Retold.

A much more widespread tale type is 1074, *Race Won by Deception: Relative Helpers*. Aarne and Thompson cite variants from Iceland to India, as well as from European-American, African-American, and Native American sources. Many variants from Asia and Africa have also been published.

The identities of the two animals who race, as well as the precise strategy of the slower competitor, vary widely. In a Japanese variant, a whale races a sea slug who shows up ahead of him on every beach in Japan. In variants from the Philippines, a deer races with a snail who appears at each waterhole the deer visits.

THE FOX AND THE CRAB/*China*

Source: Mary H. Davis and Chow Leung, *Chinese Fables and Stories*. Retold.

Another type of race is described in Tale Type 275, *The Race of the Fox and the Crayfish*. Variants have been recorded from Ireland to India, China, and Indonesia, as well as from European-American, African-American, and Native American sources.

Competitors in variants of this tale type include a fox and a lobster in a Russian tale, and a horsefly and a fox in a tale from Chile. A turtle holds onto a beaver's tail in a Seneca story, a cricket rides on Br'er Fox's tail in an Uncle Remus tale, a chameleon rides on a cheetah's tail in a story from the Kaula people of Africa, and in a Scottish tale a wren hitches a ride on an eagle's wing.

THE GUNNY WOLF/*United States: African-American*

Source: Annie Weston Whitney and Caroline Canfield Bullock, "Folk-Lore from Maryland." Retold with permission.

Not catalogued by Aarne and Thompson as a tale type, this plot combines two well-known tale motifs, K606, *Escape by singing song*, and K606.1.2, *Escape by playing sleep-bringing music*. These motifs have been recorded in Icelandic, Irish, African, and Native American tales.

The meaning of the word *gunny* in this story is not known, nor is the origin of the words in the girl's song. Do these come from another language, or are they merely nonsense? Children enjoy them anyway, and their strangeness adds to the magic of their sleep-inducing effect.

GROUNDHOG'S DANCE/*United States, Native American: Cherokee*

Source: James Mooney, "Myths of the Cherokee." Retold.

Not catalogued by Aarne and Thompson as a tale type, this story features motif K606.2, *Escape by persuading captors to dance*, which has been recorded in African, East Indian, Indonesian, and Native American tales.

The ending of this story, explaining how a long-tailed animal came to have a short tail, is extremely widespread. It is a humorous and customary way of ending a story, and not meant to be taken as fact.

THE THREE PIGS/*England*

Source: Joseph Jacobs, *English Folk & Fairy Tales*. Slightly retold.

Aarne and Thompson refer to variants of this tale (Tale Type 124, *Blowing the House In*) from England, Denmark, Ireland, France, Spain, Germany, Italy, Hungary, Yugoslavia, Turkey, and Japan, as well as from European-American and Native American sources. In other European variants, the three animals may be goats or chickens. Sometimes they are animals of three different kinds who leave their home on a farm when they learn they are to be killed and eaten.

In this version of the tale, the third pig has extra fun at the wolf's expense before doing him in. The tendency in books and films to eliminate these episodes, and to allow the first two pigs to escape the wolf (in the cartoon version by Walt Disney, for example), undermines the valuable lesson of the tale, that "wolves" are indeed dangerous and that one needs to be intelligent and diligent to succeed, or even survive, in the world.

WORKS CONSULTED

Aarne, Antti, and Stith Thompson. *The Types of the Folktale: A Classification and Bibliography.* 2nd rev. ed. Folklore Fellows Communications no. 184. Helsinki: Suomalainen Tiedeakatemia, 1961.

Afanas'ev, Aleksandr. *Russian Folk-Tales.* Translated by L. A. Magnus. New York: Dutton, 1916.

Beckwith, Martha Warren. "Jamaica Anansi Stories." *Memoirs of the American Folk-Lore Society* XVII (1924).

Beyer, Henry Otley. "Ethnography of the Bisayan Peoples." *Philippine Folklore, Customs, and Beliefs.* Manila, 1917. Typescript.

Bryant, Sara Cone. *How to Tell Stories to Children.* Boston: Houghton Mifflin, 1905.

———. *Stories to Tell to Children.* Boston: Houghton Mifflin, 1907.

Chase, Richard. *Grandfather Tales.* Boston: Houghton Mifflin, 1948.

Clarkson, Atelia, and Gilbert B. Cross. *World Folktales.* New York: Charles Scribner's Sons, 1980.

Crane, Thomas Frederick. *Italian Popular Tales.* Boston: Houghton Mifflin, 1885.

Dasent, George Webbe, ed. and trans. *Tales from the Fjeld*. Selections from the collection of Peter Christen Asbjørnsen and Jørgen Moe. New York: G. P. Putnam's Sons, 1908.

Davis, Mary H., and Chow Leung. *Chinese Fables and Stories*. New York: American Book Co., 1908.

Holbek, Bengt. "The Big-Bellied Cat." In *Varia Folklorica*, ed. by Alan Dundes. New York: Mouton, 1978.

Jacobs, Joseph. *English Folk & Fairy Tales*. New York: G. P. Putnam's Sons, 1898.

Lummis, Charles F. *Pueblo Indian Folk-Stories*. New York: Century Co., 1910.

MacDonald, Margaret Read. *The Storytellers' Sourcebook: A Subject, Title and Motif Index to Folklore Collections for Children*. Detroit: Gale/Neal-Shuman, 1982

———— *Twenty Tellable Tales: Audience Participation Folktales for the Beginning Storyteller*. Bronx, N.Y.: H. W. Wilson Company, 1986.

Mooney, James. "Myths of the Cherokee." *Report of the Bureau of American Ethnology* XIX (1897-8).

Paredes, Américo, ed. and trans. *Folktales of Mexico*. Chicago: University of Chicago Press, 1970.

Thompson, Stith. *Motif-Index of Folk-Literature*. 6 vols. Bloomington, IN: Indiana University Press, 1955-8.

Weeks, John H. *Congo Life and Folklore*. London: The Religious Tract Society, 1911.

Whitney, Annie Weston, and Caroline Canfield Bullock. "Folk-Lore from Maryland." *Memoirs of the American Folk-Lore Society* XVIII (1925).